To the children of San José,
because this is their story.
To Noella Young,
because her book inspired this one.
To Bruno, Lourdes, Carlitos and
all the people of La Urbina library
because, although they don't believe in
Utopia, they work to make a better world.

In the 1920s, when Venezuela began to export oil instead of coffee, people from the farms moved into the city. At first they were few, but in the '50s thousands came from the towns and villages to live in big cities like Caracas and Maracaibo.

The cities were not ready to receive these new inhabitants. There were no houses for them, no water works, no sewers, no electricity. And, even worse, there was not enough work for all. Many of them stayed on the outskirts of the cities in cramped shacks, uncomfortable and miserable. Sometimes they had to fight to keep their empty lots.

In Caracas, the people coming from the rural areas occupied the hills surrounding the city, hoping that some day they would live in the valley below, without fear of the landslides, with enough drinking water, without the smell of sewers and garbage. But most of them stayed there. And each year more people came. Today, almost half of the population of Caracas lives in these "barrios."

The Streets are Free is based on the true story of the children of the barrio of San José de la Urbina, who wanted a place to play. They still don't have it, but continue dreaming and fighting for their playground.

Canadian Cataloguing in Publication Data
Kurusa
    The streets are free

Translation of: La calle es libre.
ISBN 1-55037-370-6

I. Doppert, Monica. II. Title.

Z7.K87St 1994   j863   C94-931539-7

Distributed in Canada by: Published in the U.S.A. by Annick Press (U.S.) Ltd.
Firefly Books Ltd.   Distributed in the U.S.A. by:
250 Sparks Ave.   Firefly Books (U.S.) Inc.
Willowdale, ON   P.O. Box 1338
M2H 2S4   Ellicott Station
    Buffalo, NY 14205

Printed in Hong Kong

The Streets are Free

Story by Kurusa
Illustrations by Monika Doppert
Translation by Karen Englander

Annick Press Ltd.
Toronto • New York

Not very long ago, when Carlitos' grandfather was a boy, mountain lions roamed the hills of Venezuela.

One particular mountain was covered with forests and bushes, small creeks and dirt paths. Every morning the mist would reach down and touch the flowers and the butterflies.

On the hill above the town of Caracas, where Cheo, Carlitos and Camila now live, there was just one house. It was a simple house, made of mud and dried leaves from sugar cane and banana plants. In the mornings, when the family went to fetch water, they often saw lions' tracks in the soft earth. Later, they would stop by the creeks to catch sardines for dinner.

Years passed and more people came from towns and villages all over Venezuela to make their homes on the mountainside.

They built their houses of wood, and the children played among the trees, in the creeks and in the open fields.

The forest began to grow towards the new village, and the village began to grow towards the forest.

The dirt road that led to the big city was soon covered with asphalt.

And more people came.

There were so many houses that they reached right to the top of the mountain where the lion tracks used to be. The creeks became sewers. The dirt paths were littered with garbage. The mountain became a very poor town called the "barrio" San José.

The children who used to play in the open fields could no longer play there, nor in the forest, nor in the streams.

The fields in the valleys were now filled with office towers. The whole mountain was covered with houses. The main road became a highway. There were only a few trees and not one flower.

The children had nowhere to play.

After school, Cheo, Carlitos and Camila went to a house that had been converted into a library. There they read books, and played with clay and paints and boardgames and all kinds of interesting things. But they had nowhere to play hopscotch, or soccer, or baseball, or tag.

After they left the library, they played in the street.

One day, while they were playing leapfrog, a grocery truck came barrelling down the street. The driver shouted:

"Get out of the way! Let me through!"

"The streets are free," said the boys. But the truck was much bigger and more powerful than the children. So they walked to the top of the mountain to fly their kites. In about half an hour, every one of the kites was tangled in the hydro wires.

The children went back down the mountain to play ball. But the ball kept getting lost in people's washing, and trapped on roof tops.

One woman ran out of her house when the children were trying to fetch the ball.

"Get out of here," she shouted, "or I'll hit you with my broom."

"The streets are free," said the youngest boy. But the children knew they had better leave her alone.

Dejected, they went to the library. They sat down on the steps and thought.

"There must be somewhere we can play," said Camila.

"Let's go see the mayor and tell him we need somewhere to play," suggested another.

"Where does he live?" asked Carlitos, the smallest boy. The children looked at each other. Nobody knew.

"Let's go to City Hall. That can't be too far away."

"But we can't go there without adults. They won't listen to us at City Hall," said Camila, with big, sad eyes.

"Then let's ask our parents."

So the children went from house to house to ask their parents to go with them to City Hall.

But their parents were...

....cooking,
sewing,
washing,
repairing,
away working,
in other words... busy.

The children returned to the library steps. They just sat there, and felt very sad.

Then the librarian appeared.

"Why all the sad faces?" he asked.

The children told him.

"What do you want to tell the mayor?"

"We want a playground."

"Do you know where?"

"Yes," said Carlitos, "in an empty lot near the bottom of the mountain."

"Do you know what it should look like?"

"Well..."

"Why don't you come inside and discuss it?"

They talked for more than an hour. Cheo, the oldest boy, took notes on a large pad.

"Good," said the librarian, "and now what do you want to do?"

"We're still in the same boat," said Camila. "What good is a piece of paper if the adults don't go with us to see the mayor?"

"Won't they go with you?"

"They won't even listen to us," Camila said.

"Have you tried going alone?"

"Well, no."

"So, what do you want to do?"

The children looked at each other.

"Let's make a banner," said Cheo.

They all worked together and made a sign that said:

WE HAVE NOWHERE TO PLAY
WE NEED A PLAYGROUND

"Tomorrow we'll plan the details," said the librarian, and he left for the chess club.

The children put the finishing touches on their sign.

"It's perfect like this!"

They rolled up the sign and the large list with their notes.

"We're ready," they said.

Again the children looked at each other. "Why don't we go right now?" a few children said at the same time.

With the banner and the large list of notes rolled up under their arms, the children of San José walked to City Hall.

City Hall was even bigger than they had imagined. The doorway was very high. Standing in the middle of it was a big, fat man.

"No one comes in here," he said.

"We came to ask for a playground."

"We came to see the people at City Hall. We need a playground."

"But the people at the Council don't want to see you. Go home or I'll call the police."

"Look, this is the kind of playground we want," said Carlitos innocently, and he unrolled the paper with their notes on it.

Camila said, "We need somewhere to play," and she unrolled the banner.

"Get out of here!" shouted the fat man.

"The streets are free!" Cheo shouted back, and sat down.

"We're not going to move until they listen to us," said another boy. "In the library they told us that City Hall is here to listen to us."

Back in San José, the mothers were worried. They couldn't find their children. Somebody said she had seen them leaving the library with some big sheets of paper.

"Oh, no," mumbled the librarian. "I think I know where they are."

The fat man in the doorway of City Hall was
yelling so much that his face was turning redder and
redder. A crowd gathered around City Hall to see what all
the fuss was about.

Then everything happened at once. The mothers, the librarian and
the police all arrived at City Hall at the same time.

The mothers shouted, "What are you doing?"

"Take them away!" shouted the fat man to the police. "They're disturbing the peace." The policemen started pulling the children by their arms.

"Excuse me," the librarian raised one hand, "but what is going on here?"

"They won't let us talk to anyone about our playground," said Carlitos.

"The police are going to arrest them and put them in jail for their bad behaviour," said the fat man.

Then one mother, who was even bigger and fatter than he, stood in front of the children.

"Oh, no, you don't," she said. "If you put a hand on these kids, you have to arrest me, too."

"And me, too," said another mother.

"And me," shouted the rest of the mothers.

Suddenly, standing in the doorway of City Hall, was the mayor, a reporter and a municipal engineer.

"What's going on here?" the mayor asked.

"We need a playground."

"They want to arrest us."

"Those people are starting a riot."

They were all talking at once.

"Let the children speak," the librarian suggested.

"Yes, I'd like to talk to the children," said the reporter, getting out her notebook. They told her their story.

When they were finished, the mayor turned to the municipal engineer. "Is there space for them to have a playground?"

"Yes!" the children shouted together. "We know where. We can show you."

"Why don't you come and see it?" asked the librarian.

"Um—" said the engineer.

"Uhmmmmmmm—" said the mayor. "Tomorrow. Tomorrow we'll look at it. I don't have time now. I'm very busy. But tomorrow, tomorrow for sure. Ahem. Remember, we are here to serve you." Then the mayor shook hands with all the mothers.

"I knew it," said Camila.

We need a playground
with trees
and shrubs
and flower seeds
swings
an old tractor to climb on
and sticks to dig with
A house for dolls
a lasso to play cowboys
Lots of room for baseball
volleyball and soccer,
to have races and
fly kites,
to play leapfrog, tag,
kick-the-can,
blind man's bluff
and hide and seek
grass to roll on
and do gymnastics
A patio to play on
and a bench
for our parents
to sit and visit.
THE END

"I would very much like to go with you," said the reporter. So the children, the mothers, the librarian and the reporter all went to see the empty lot.

"What do you want the playground to look like?" the reporter asked. The children began to read their list. The reporter took lots of notes and wrote down everything on their sign:

The next day, the library was empty. The children sat on the steps.

"I think," sighed Camila, "I think that nothing's going to happen."

"What if we went to City Hall again with our big brothers and sisters?" asked Carlitos.

"They'll put us in jail," Camila said.

A week passed.

One day, the librarian appeared in the doorway, smiling. He was holding a newspaper with a huge headline:

THE CHILDREN OF SAN JOSÉ TAKE ON CITY HALL

They ask for special park
The mayor doesn't come through

"That's us!" said Cheo.

"We're famous!" laughed Carlitos.

"Yeah, but they're still not going to do anything," said Camila.

She was wrong. The same afternoon, the mayor, the municipal engineer and three assistants came to the barrio.

"We came to see the land for the playground. Soon we'll give it to you," they said proudly.

"Very soon," said the engineer.

"Very, very soon," smiled the mayor.

This Site Reserved For

THE CHILDREN'S PARK
OF SAN JOSÉ

Then it happened: one morning, the assistants tied a red ribbon across the entrance to the empty lot. At twelve o'clock sharp, the mayor, dressed very elegantly and with freshly-shined shoes, came and cut the ribbon with an extra-large pair of scissors.

"I get it," said Camila, "there's an election soon, isn't there? After the big ceremony, I'll bet nothing will happen."

This time Camila was right. Weeks passed and the engineers never came back. The empty lot that was supposed to be the playground was just collecting garbage. Little by little, the adults forgot about it. But the children didn't.

"What happened to our playground?" the children asked. The adults always gave the same answer:

"The politicians always promise, but they never do anything."

Carlitos, Camila and Cheo weren't satisfied. They sat on the edge of the mountain and looked down at the empty lot and thought about it all.

Then Carlitos said, "Why can't we have a playground anyway?"

"Are you crazy? It's very complicated."

"But if everybody helped, maybe..."

It was a crazy idea, but the younger children started talking to their friends, who talked to their older brothers and sisters, who talked to their mothers, and the mothers talked to the fathers.

One day, Carlitos heard his uncle and some friends arguing about the playground. His uncle banged the table. He said they could easily build the playground themselves—they didn't need the council. But his friends were not so sure.

"Don't be crazy. Nobody co-operates here, not even to clean up the sidewalk! How could you get everyone to build them a playground?"

"No, buddy, everyone knows each other. They'll help," said Carlitos' uncle.

"Forget it. You'll end up building it yourself."

"Alone? No. I'll help you," said one of the men.

"I will, too."

Time passed and more and more people talked about the idea. The neighbourhood committee organized a public meeting one Saturday. About fifty people came. The discussion lasted four hours and was very loud.

"We can't do it," said some.

"We can do it," said others.

There seemed no way to agree. Carlitos' uncle and the children passionately defended the idea, but most of the parents doubted it could be done without the politicians' help.

After all the shouting, there was silence. It looked like the meeting was going to end that way, until one mother remembered that she had some planks of wood she didn't need. One father said he was a carpenter. One girl timidly said, "In my house we have some rope to make a swing with."

Everybody became very enthusiastic and suddenly they all had suggestions.

"I want to bring some nails," insisted one grandmother.

Carlitos, Cheo and Camila all started jumping up and down.

"It's really going to happen!"

HURRAY!

All the neighbours began to build the playground.
They brought cement and bricks and buckets and sheets of
aluminum and sandbags and old tires and wooden boards of every size.

They nailed and hammered and
dug holes and planted and sanded.
They all worked in their spare time...

On the wire fence the children put up a sign they had made themselves:

SAN JOSÉ PLAYGROUND
EVERYBODY COME
AND PLAY